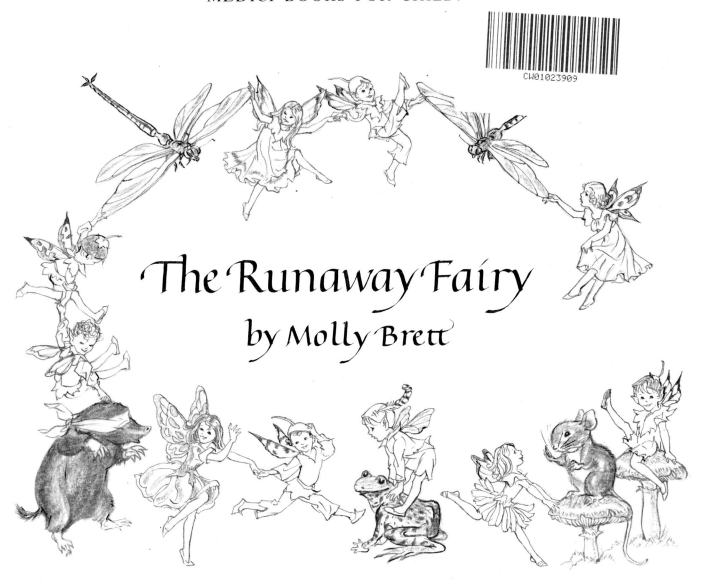

The Runaway Fairy
by Molly Brett

© The Medici Society Ltd., London, 1982. Printed in England. ISBN 0 85503 066 6. B66

Every plant and bush in the garden belonged to a fairy, elf, or pixie, each caring for their own particular flowers, watering them with dewdrops, supporting stems when winds were rough, and chasing off caterpillars, slugs, and snails.

A lovely rose bush grew in the garden and this belonged to the Fairy Rosalind. Proudly she watched over her flowers and only the butterflies and bumblebees were allowed near. Ordinary bees in search of honey were not welcome, 'You will disarrange the petals!' she scolded, chasing them off.

One day Rosalind was very annoyed to find that a large dandelion had appeared close to her bush. 'What a horrid WEED!' she cried and quickly called some elves to pull it out, while nearby pansies stared at the intruder with frowns on their pretty faces, and the snapdragons snapped their jaws so fiercely that a small elf got caught by mistake.

Then early one morning a dreadful thing happened when Rosalind was awakened by a strange and terrible sound: CLIP! SNIP! CLIP! SNIP! and saw to her horror that all her roses were being snipped off to go to the local flower show.

The rose fairy was heartbroken and the other fairies tried to comfort her, 'You may share my flowers,' said Lucy Love-in-a-mist kindly. 'Your roses will grow again,' Laura Lily told her, while Polly Poppy suggested rather tactlessly, 'Perhaps you could take over something in the vegetable garden—try a cauliflower.'

But Rosalind wailed, 'Now I have no flowers of my own to look after I shall run away and visit my cousins the Wild Flower Fairies who live in the country; I am sure it is a much more exciting place than this dull garden.' Then she spread her wings and flew over the hedge.

As she went she asked passing birds the way to the countryside and, following their directions, flew on and on until her wings ached. Then, alighting to rest, she saw that there were fields and woods all round her and knew that she had reached the country.

Hearing a loud buzzing she saw a fluffy bumble bee caught in a spider's web and hastened to rescue him. She would then have flown on but found that *her* feet were stuck to the ground! Rosalind had stepped on a Sundew plant and its sticky leaves held her feet fast.

4

Her cry for help brought the bee hurrying up and he, calling on other insects, soon pulled her free, but—she lost her slippers.

Then, hearing a little snoring sound, she peeped round a clump of heather and saw a hedgehog lying there fast asleep, while creeping up to twist itself round his neck was . . . a snake!

'Wake up! Quick! Wake up!' warned Rosalind and, as the snake was about to dart forward, the fairy seized a fircone lying near and threw it as hard as she could. Her aim was good and the cone hit him on the head so that he wriggled away in a hurry while the hedgehog, who had rolled himself into a prickly ball, slowly uncurled and thanked the fairy for his rescue.

Rosalind asked him where she might find some of the Wild Flower Fairies. 'They are giving a party today for animal friends and all are welcome,' grunted the hedgehog, so they set off together and were soon joined by other animals all hurrying to the party: mice in well polished fur coats and with curly whiskers, rabbits with flowers in their ears, and squirrels whose fine tails were decorated with daisy chains.

The hedgehog sighed and looked so sad that Rosalind asked what was the matter. 'They are all very smart,' he grunted, 'but *my* prickles always look untidy and nobody will want to sit next to me at the party.'

'I will,' promised Rosalind loyally though he did look rather spiky, 'and we can decorate your prickles just like the others.' This was soon done and the hedgehog cheered up as they hurried on to a secret green glade; excited twitterings, squeaks, and grunts came from it with the fairies' picnic all set out on a large lace tablecloth of cobwebs and skeleton leaves.

Rosalind was introduced to the Wild Flower Fairies and told them that several of their relations lived in her garden—Diana Daisy heard of Sunflowers, Marguerites, Michaelmas Daisies and many others in her flower family.

Vera Vetch was told about her Sweetpea Aunt who wore such lovely colours, and Toby Toadflax was proud to hear of his uncle Snapdragon, while Rosalind was delighted to meet her own little cousin Baby Briar Rose.

But Dandy the Dandelion elf was not at all pleased. 'When *my* flowers try to grow in gardens they are *pulled up* and called WEEDS so . . . does that happen in *your* garden?' he snapped at Rosalind who had to admit that it did.

Dandy tossed his mop of yellow hair, of which he was very proud, and muttered, 'We don't want any stuck-up garden fairies here,' calling up his pet wasp to drive Rosalind away. But Tom Teazel and Ragged Robin chased it off and invited her to join in the games of musical chairs with the mice, leapfrog, blindman's buff, and hide-and-seek. Can you see where the fairies hid?

Then the fairies had a dance over the stream with the dragonflies and a kingfisher,

and they went water ski-ing pulled along by a moorhen.

Meanwhile Dandy, jealous at seeing how popular Rosalind was becoming with the other fairies, decided to play tricks on her and as she came whizzing downstream in fine style he threw a fat worm into the water in front of the moorhen, who suddenly stood on its head to grab it and poor Rosalind got a ducking. However a kindly frog came to her rescue and she was soon dry again in the sunshine.

Then the squirrels offered her a swing but Dandy Dandelion jeered, 'Can't you go higher than that?' and whispered to the squirrels, 'Chuck her off!'. So when Rosalind called 'Push harder,' they promptly sent the swing so high that she fell off into a bramble bush and tore her dress.

Then it was time for the grand Rabbit Race and the rose fairy was thrilled at the chance of riding a real rabbit as there were none in her own garden.

All the rabbits were very frisky and there was great excitement as the race started.

Bessy Buttercup, who was rather a fat fairy, bounced so high on her mount that she landed in an overhanging bramble, little Ragged Robin fell into a gorse bush, Frank Foxglove's rabbit was chased by a weasel, while Diana Daisy disappeared down a rabbit hole. Other elves and fairies tumbled off and soon Rosalind and Dandy were well ahead, leaping over tufts of heather and across the stream they went side by side, until suddenly that mean dandelion elf threw a tasty wild strawberry just in front of Rosalind's mount—but the rabbit *he* was riding saw it first, stopped to nibble and Dandy fell off while the rose fairy raced on to win amid much applause.

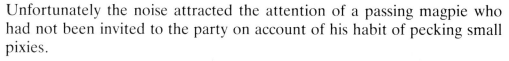

Unfortunately the noise attracted the attention of a passing magpie who had not been invited to the party on account of his habit of pecking small pixies.

Now magpies love bright things and, seeing the shining wings and gay clothes of the little people, he swooped down and seized one with bright yellow hair—none other than Dandy Dandelion.

Although he had tried to play tricks on her the rose fairy could not help feeling sorry for poor Dandy caught in that cruel black beak, and before the magpie could fly off she cried, 'We must rescue him!' and seized the end of his long tail.

The other fairies joined her and away they went up into the air, the magpie twisting and flapping and even turning somersaults in his efforts to shake them off, while small birds from the party hurried up to join in the chase and Rosalind held on tight to his tail. At last he squawked, 'Let go! let go! you will pull off my tail!' and as he opened his beak Dandy wriggled free, the feather to which the rose fairy had been clinging broke off, and she and the others fluttered down safely to be welcomed by their animal friends at the party.

But the dandelion elf had had such a fright that his yellow hair turned white, like a seedhead. Then the wind blew it all away leaving him quite bald and obliged to wear a hat until it grew again.

It was now evening and time for a dance in the fairy ring while dormice and frogs made music, the nightingale sang, an owl hooted, and cockchafers hummed for Rosalind to dance with her friends until dawn.

The visit to the Wild Flower Fairies had certainly been exciting, but now Rosalind was ready to return to her own quiet garden to tell of her adventures and wait for her own roses to grow again.

But her dress was torn, her slippers lost, and her hair in a tangle; such an untidy fairy would not be welcome in her own neat garden. So the Wild Flower Fairies all gave petals to make her a new dress sewn by Sarah Stichwort, the Lady's Slipper pixie made her new shoes, and Helen Hairbell cared for her hair.

After saying good-bye to all her friends, Rosalind flew away towards her own garden and, as she came to a large field near the town, saw that flags were flying and there was a big tent with a crowd of people waiting to go in. The flower show was about to begin and Rosalind flew down to see. She slipped through a gap in the tent and, peeping inside, saw that it was full of flowers, fruit, and vegetables, with a nice smell of newly cut grass underfoot, and soon Rosalind had met several other fairies from gardens near her own.

Some of them were very excited. 'My marrow is the biggest,' boasted a fat pixie; 'My flowers have won second prize,' said Priscilla Pansy, while another elf was proudly polishing his tomatoes which had been given third prize . . . but Rosalind looked in vain for her own roses which had been snipped off for the show.

Then on a platform at the end of the tent she saw a big silver cup on a table. In front of it was a vase and in it . . . were her very own roses next to a big red card with FIRST PRIZE and CHAMPION OF THE SHOW printed on it.

People were now crowding into the tent and the fairies disappeared quickly into their own gardens. But Rosalind was too late and as she tried to escape a little boy with sharp eyes saw her.

'Oooh, what a big butterfly!' he shouted and gave chase and as the fairy fluttered out of the tent he threw his sun hat on top of her. Up came his sister and they peeped under the hat.

'Why it's a fairy—a real fairy!' exclaimed the little girl. 'No, its a big butterfly,' said the boy.

'I shall invite her to stay in my dolls' house and have tea with the dolls,' said his sister. '*I* shall take it to school for nature class,' insisted her brother and then... a gust of wind caught the sun hat blowing it away over the grass and up into the air, while Rosalind flew off to her own garden safe at last.

That evening she told the story of her adventures at a grand garden party with a procession of Chinese lanterns, and all the fairies peeping through the window of the house to see her prize-winning roses and the grand silver cup, which the proud owners had brought back in triumph after the show.

Very soon her rose bush grew new buds and she was busy again chasing off ants, greenfly, and caterpillars, and hoping there would be no more snipping and clipping. On Midsummer Eve she visits the Wild Flower Fairies again as they are too shy to come to her garden, but Dandy keeps away in case he and his dandelions get PULLED UP. Instead they make the roadsides gay for many who have no gardens; so Dandy, although rather a naughty elf, does do one good deed after all.